Lily's Christmas Promise

Maryse Dawson

Published by Maryse Dawson, 2024.

This is a work of fiction. Similarities to real people, places, or events are entirely coincidental.

LILY'S CHRISTMAS PROMISE

First edition. November 6, 2024.

Copyright © 2024 Maryse Dawson.

ISBN: 979-8231248575

Written by Maryse Dawson.

Also by Maryse Dawson

Pirates Quest
Tides of Desire (Pirates Quest Book 1)
The Pirates Quest Collection
Captive to the Heart

Standalone
Taming the Willful Miss Roberts
Between Duty and Desire
Scandal in Silk: A Victorian Love Affair
Lily's Christmas Promise
A Passion for Annie

Watch for more at https://www.facebook.com/maryse.dawson.5.

Chapter One

Whispering Pines 1879

The winter sun hung low in the sky, casting long shadows over the snow-laden trees as a lone figure rode into Whispering Pines. His tall, muscular frame sat atop a majestic black stallion, the only sound in the crisp air the soft jingle of the horse's bridle. He could see the curtains twitch as the townsfolk watched him, no doubt whispering among themselves as to who he could be.

But it was nothing he wasn't used to.

He'd been wandering around for the past five years or so, trying to settle yet never seeming to find the right place—his tormented soul finding no respite.

Ever since his wife, Carrie, had died from pneumonia, he'd been filled with grief, and the only way he knew how to deal with it was to move on. To somehow try and find a new life, a new beginning. But nothing seemed to be working.

His chest tightened at the thought of her, and he tried to push the feeling aside. As the years passed, it was getting easier. He'd hardened himself to grief. But he would never forget.

At the edge of town, nestled among the snow-covered fields, stood the large ranch of the Montgomery family. He reined in his horse, Nyx, and sat for a moment to regard the area. It was quiet and serene. Just his sort of place.

He'd been drawn by the promise of solitude and a fresh start. It seemed John Montgomery hadn't lied. The man had advertised for an able-bodied, strong man willing to help about the ranch. In return for a warm bed, meals, his own accommodation, and a decent wage.

It was just what he was looking for.

He regarded the main house. It was a grand structure of weathered wood and stone. There was a wide porch, the length of the building, and several fenced-off areas surrounding it holding quite a few horses. In the distance, cattle grazed on the grass, their noses pushing through the thin snow covering to find sustenance.

He closed his eyes for a moment and let the peace settle over him. Yes, this was exactly what he needed. He urged his horse forward, the animal's breath misting in the cold air.

• • ❧ • •

Around the back of the big house, Lily Montgomery was busy mending a fence under the watchful eye of her father. Her fiery spirit and determination were evident in the way she handled the tools, her laughter ringing out gaily in the winter air.

"Don't swing it so hard, Lily." Her father cautioned. "You'll be the first to winge if you catch a finger."

"Oh, pa! Ain't no trouble. Look!"

She swung the hammer up and bashed it down on the new partition, giving a triumphant smile when it went straight into the ground. "You see. I'm quite capable."

"Hmmm." He said, pursing his lips. "The sooner Ethan Blackwood gets here, the better. Women shouldn't have to do this sort of thing. It's men's work."

Lily placed her hands on her hips. "Men's work! Really, pa. This ain't the sixteen hundreds, you know."

As she paused to wipe a strand of blonde hair from her face, her gaze caught sight of a stranger approaching their land.

Curiosity mingled with caution in her emerald eyes as she observed the newcomer, his dark silhouette a stark contrast against the white landscape. She felt a flutter of unease in her chest, a sensation she couldn't quite explain. The man seemed awfully big.

"Pa, is that the man you're expecting?"

Her father turned his head and studied him. "Only one way to find out, Lily." He held his hand up and waved. The stranger dismounted his horse with a grace that belied his rugged appearance, his dark eyes looking across to them.

Lily watched quietly from a distance. As the cowboy approached, a faint smile played on his lips. Lord, he was handsome. His hair was dark brown, just reaching the nape of his neck, and he had a neatly trimmed, thick beard. He was not only tall but broad-shouldered, and his long legs, clad in blue jeans, were muscular and defined.

His hazel eyes settled on hers for a moment, and she found she couldn't look away.

Her father greeted him with a firm handshake, his weathered face beaming as he exchanged pleasantries. "Ethan?"

"Yes, Sir. Ethan Blackwood." His deep voice drawled in the winter air, and Lily found she still couldn't tear her gaze away. He was gorgeous.

"John Montgomery." Her father replied, and then turning to Lily, he introduced her, "And my daughter, Lily."

"Howdy, miss."

His piercing eyes seemed to see right through her, and she felt her face grow hot as she replied, "Hello."

"We've just about finished here." Her father said, "We were just putting in some new posts. Darn critters gnawed the bottom of this one."

Ethan chuckled and exposed his even white teeth. Lily was transfixed, feeling an instant tug of desire. Wow. She turned around and busied herself with picking up the tools they'd used—anything to hide her flaming cheeks. She hadn't felt such an attraction to a man in ages and never one so instantaneous either.

"Come to the house, and we'll settle you in." She heard her father say, "My wife's made meat pie for dinner tonight; you arrived at just the right time."

"Can I help you with that, Lily?" Ethan hunkered down next to her, and when she raised her eyes to his, they were only inches away. Damn! She swallowed hard. "No, thank you. I've just about finished."

"Well, let me carry the bag for you," he offered.

Her eyes flashed back to his. "I'm perfectly capable of carrying a bag. Thank you all the same."

Her father laughed. "One thing you have to learn, Ethan, is that my daughter is very independent."

She watched Ethan raise an eyebrow, and he shrugged. "I'll have to remember that for next time."

The three of them turned and walked towards the main house, Ethan leading his big black stallion, who walked sedately beside them, obviously well-trained. Her father showed Ethan where to stable his horse, whilst Lily made her way indoors.

Her mother was in the kitchen, fussing over the dinner, and had her apron on.

"Ma, that new ranch hand's arrived." Lily said, reaching over and helping herself to a small raw carrot.

"Oh? Already." She glanced over to the stove. "Thank the Lord, I made enough food."

Lily sniggered, "You always do."

"What's he like?"

Lily tilted her head. "Tall, strong, and good-looking. In fact, very appealing."

"Oh, taken your fancy, has he?" Her mother laughed. "I just hope he knows what he's taking on if he returns the feeling."

"Ma! That ain't fair. Just because I believe in being independent doesn't mean to say I ain't capable of lovin' a man."

Her mother picked up a pile of carrots and put them in the saucepan. "So, how's that working out for you so far, my love?"

Lily huffed under her breath. "Not so good, but none of the men I've dated have had any gumption."

It was true. She'd only dated a few men, but none of the relationships had lasted very long. They were either too gruff or too weak. No one had really caught her eye. Until now.

Her eyes sparkled with interest as she thought of Ethan. Would he be able to handle an independent woman?

Lily's mother, Martha greeted Ethan warmly when they were introduced. "Dinner won't be long. Lily can show you the accommodation whilst I set the table."

"As long as it's no bother. I can find it myself if you point me in the right direction." He offered.

"No, no! Lily will show you, won't you, dear?" her mother said, looking at Lily expectantly.

He noticed there was a slight hesitation before Lily replied, but it was only momentary. "Sure."

He remained silent and followed her out of the kitchen, back outside, and then on towards a small log cabin further up the lane. He kept his stride slow so she could keep up.

She was a pretty little thing. Dazzling emerald green eyes, long blonde hair, and a neat little curvy figure. She had a cute butt as well. He'd always been a butt and legs man. Couldn't help himself.

They reached the cabin, and turning the key in the lock, she opened the door wide and stepped inside.

"Here you go," she said. "You've got a bedroom, a small kitchen if you need it, and the living room's in here. There's an outhouse just out the back; you can't miss it." She showed him quickly around and then stood staring at him, with her arms crossed over her chest. "You ain't got much luggage, have you?" She said to him, eyeing his carpet bag and roll pack.

"A cowboy doesn't need much." He smiled, dumping them on the kitchen floor.

She narrowed her eyes. "You on the run from someone?"

He blinked in surprise. "No. I just travel light." He crossed his arms over his chest and frowned. "You're quite direct, aren't you?"

She flushed a little. "Not always, only when I'm curious. Ain't nothin' wrong with that!"

She was getting defensive, and he couldn't help the smile that broke out on his face. "No, I don't suppose there is."

Her jaw tightened when she realised he was laughing at her, so he changed the subject. "Is there a water pump?"

"Yeah, out the back near the outhouse. There's some handmade soap and towels in the bedroom for you." She turned to leave, throwing over her shoulder, "Dinner's usually at seven."

The door clicked behind her as she left. She was a prickly little thing, and he sensed a fiery temper beneath that thin, polite veneer she wore. He gave a low, calculated smile, wondering how long it would take to show itself.

In the five long years he'd been travelling, he hadn't come across a woman that had intrigued him so much or that he'd felt such an attraction to. Staying on the ranch was going to prove interesting, that was for sure.

. . ⚘ . .

That evening, as the sun dipped below the horizon, casting a warm glow over the snow-covered landscape, Ethan arrived for dinner. Lily's eyes swept over him, noticing he'd changed his attire since earlier and was now wearing a smart shirt beneath a leather waistcoat and black trousers. He smelled good too. She loved a man that wore cologne.

He straightened his collar and ran a hand through his dark hair as she led him into the cozy dining room. He was so big, he suddenly made the room seem small.

Her parents were already gathered around the sturdy wooden table, along with her younger sister, Mary, and the aroma of a hearty meal filled the air.

Her mother smiled at him, "Take a seat, Ethan. I bet you're starving after your journey."

He nodded. "In all truth, ma'am, I haven't had a proper home-cooked meal in ages."

As he settled into his seat, Lily's father introduced him to her sister, Mary. "This is my youngest daughter, Mary. Mary, this is Ethan Blackwood. He's going to be working here for a while."

Mary grinned at him. "Do you like cards, Mr. Blackwood? I love playing cards. We could play together."

"Now, Mary. Ethan's only just arrived. Give him time to settle in," her father said. "Pass the bread rolls along."

Mary's face fell, but she immediately did as her father said and passed the basket of freshly baked bread rolls to Ethan. He smiled as he took it off her and said, "I'm sure we'll get plenty of time to play cards together. Maybe not tonight though."

Lily watched her sister grin. She was easily pleased. There was a big age gap between them. Mary was only twelve, half her age. She had been a bit of a surprise for her parents, who thought they would only ever have one child. Fate had deemed that not to be the case.

She was a little rascal but they all loved her dearly.

As her mother began to dish out the pie, the conversation flowed easily, filled with tales of ranch life and the beauty of the winter season. Her father raised his glass in a toast to their guest, his eyes studying Ethan with a keen gaze. "So, Ethan, what made you decide to take this job? Have you been to Whispering Pines before?" he inquired, his voice gruff but not unkind. Her father was a very direct man. A trait Lily had inherited.

Ethan met her father's gaze with a steady look, the flickering firelight casting shadows across his rugged features. "No, I've never been here before. The truth is, I've been travelling around for the last five years," he began, his voice tinged with a hint of melancholy. "My wife died five years ago, and ever since I've been drifting from town to town."

"Oh, I'm so sorry to hear that," her mother said. "What a terrible thing to happen. May I ask how she died?"

"Pneumonia. She got caught in the rain. That was all it took." He shook his head, his eyes gazing into the fire. "Life's very fragile."

Her mother's gentle eyes softened with compassion as she listened. "That must have been a very hard time for you." Her hand reached out and patted his arm. "You're welcome to stay with us for as long as you need."

"Indeed you are, Ethan." Her father added. "I can't begin to imagine what you've been through, but hopefully you'll find some peace here at the ranch."

Lily's eyes widened with empathy, her heart aching for the pain that lay hidden beneath Ethan's stoic exterior. She was amazed he could smile at all. "I can show you the cattle tomorrow if you like." she offered. "We could take a ride out."

He turned to look at her and nodded. "I would like that."

"Well, now, let's clear these plates away and we'll get dessert served out." Her mother stood up, and Mary and Lily passed the plates along.

"We've got apple pie with cream." Mary grinned at Ethan. "Do you like apples, Mr. Blackwood?"

"Very much."

That night, when Lily got ready for bed, she couldn't stop thinking about Ethan. She felt a deep sadness for him but also a deep set desire.

Putting her long blonde hair in a tight plait, she pulled the covers aside and then slipped beneath the cozy fabric, moving her legs about to try and create some warmth.

Mary was watching her from her own bed, her eyes sparkling with excitement. "I like Mr. Blackwood. Do you?"

"You only like him because he said he'd play cards with you." Lily reasoned, smiling. "No, in all truth, I do like him. He seems like a very nice man."

"Do you think you'll marry him?"

"What?!" Lily spluttered, her mouth agape. "What on earth makes you think that?"

"Well, why not? He's handsome, and he was looking at you a lot tonight."

"No, he wasn't. Was he?"

Mary nodded, her eyes wide and full of mischief.

Lily sat up in bed and pointed a finger at her. "If you're lyin' you'll go straight to hell. Remember what the preacher said about lyin'!"

Mary pulled a face. "I ain't lyin', honest, Lily. I just find it nice that he thinks you're pretty. I think you're pretty."

Lily's heart softened, and she was immediately contrite for snapping at her. "Ah, that's sweet of you to say, Mary. I think you're pretty too." She settled back down on her pillow. "Now, get some sleep."

It didn't take long for Mary to fall asleep; Lily could hear her even breathing. For Lily, not so much. A pair of handsome hazel eyes kept coming to mind, as did the smell of his masculine cologne. Lord, he'd only just arrived, and he was getting under her skin!

Chapter Two

The next day dawned crisp and clear, the sun casting a golden hue over the snow-covered fields of the Montgomery ranch. Lily saddled her chestnut mare, her heart fluttering with anticipation as she prepared to show Ethan the expanse of their cattle ranch. Dressed in figure-hugging jeans, her favourite riding gear, although her father highly disapproved, she awaited his arrival outside the front of the ranch, a sense of excitement bubbling in her chest.

She kept thinking about what her sister had said last night—that Ethan had kept looking at her. That must mean he liked her. Surely.

As Ethan emerged from the stables leading his horse, his dark gaze met Lily's, and he shot her a slow smile. "I haven't kept you waiting, have I?"

"No. I'd soon let you know if you had." She replied sassily, grinning.

He raised an eyebrow. "Like that, is it?"

"Yep!" She laughed.

They mounted their horses and set off towards the fields, the crunch of hooves on snow mingling with the whisper of the wind through the trees. The vast expanse of the ranch unfolded before them, dotted with grazing cattle and fields of thoroughbred horses.

Dismounting near a sturdy fence that overlooked the rolling hills, Lily waited for Ethan to join her.

"Well? What do you think?" She asked him, her breath misting in the cold air.

"It's beautiful, but I can see why you need some help. This is a lot of land to upkeep." He stood next to her, his large hands on the top rung of the fence as he looked around. "I heard there was hired help here before, but he left." His eyes settled on hers as he angled his head to look at her.

Close up; she could see the flecks in the hazel depths, and there was a sincerity in his eyes that you didn't see very often. She felt her heart flutter.

"Adam used to work here, but he got married and moved onto his own ranch." She pointed a finger at a house in the distance. "See that house there; that's his. He still pops by, but he has enough to do, maintaining his own place."

"How come you aren't married? If you don't mind me asking?"

Her eyes shot to his, and she flushed a little. "Because I ain't found anyone I like."

. . ∾ . .

Ethan watched the colour rise in her cheeks and wondered if he'd touched on a nerve. But he was genuinely interested. She was damn pretty, and by her age, she looked to be about twenty-four or five; she was certainly old enough to be hitched and have a couple of children hanging onto her skirts.

Not that she was wearing skirts. Clad in the tight jeans, it didn't leave much to the imagination, and her butt looked real good. Damn good.

Suddenly, his sharp gaze caught movement in the branches above them. His instincts on high alert, he whispered, "Lily, don't move."

She looked up in surprise, her eyes widening at the sight of a majestic cougar perched on a branch above her, its golden eyes fixed on her with a predatory gleam.

"It's just a cougar, Ethan," Lily said nonchalantly, rolling her eyes at his concern. "We get them here all the time. They're usually more frightened of us." She moved nearer to take a good look at it.

Ethan's frown deepened as he observed the big cat's behaviour. "Not this one. It doesn't seem too friendly," he muttered, his hand instinctively moving to his holster.

Before Lily could react, the cougar leaped from the tree with a menacing growl, its sleek body hurtling towards her with lethal grace. In a split second, Ethan was by her side, his strong arms pulling her out of harm's way just as the predator landed where she'd stood only moments before.

"Damnation!" she shrieked, clinging onto him. He pushed her behind him and stood facing the angry cougar.

It paced back and forth, its gaze locked on them with hungry intent. Ethan didn't waste a minute; he pulled out his gun and fired at the ground right next to the animal. It was enough to scare it. As the echoes of the gunshot faded into the distance, the cougar darted off into the wilderness, growling menacingly.

.. ⚬⚬ ..

Lily felt a rush of gratitude towards Ethan. She'd encountered cougars before, but never once had they tried to attack her like that! I mean, she had a healthy fear of them, but usually they were more afraid of her than she of them!

She realised she was still holding onto his massive arms and quickly extricated herself from his grasp, her cheeks flushed with a mixture of adrenaline and shock.

"God, that was a close call. I ain't ever seen one that angry before! Usually they just keep their distance."

Ethan's dark eyes bore into hers, his jaw set in a firm line. Lily stared back at him frowning. Why was he so mad all of a sudden?

"Lily, I won't tolerate that kind of language," he said, his voice low and controlled. "I don't want to hear it again."

Lily bristled at his authoritative tone, her fiery spirit rising to meet his steely gaze. So he was pissed at her because she cussed! Seriously? "It's none of your business how I speak," she retorted, her green eyes flashing with defiance.

She saw a flicker of frustration cross Ethan's handsome face, and he fixed his eyes on her. "It is my business when we're out here in the wild, facing dangers like that," he stated firmly. "I won't have you putting yourself at risk with reckless behaviour and foul language."

Lily squared her shoulders and met Ethan's gaze head-on. "What reckless behaviour? How was I reckless?"

"When I told you to stay still, you didn't."

"Well, no, but..."

"No buts, Lily. You disobeyed me when danger was present. Don't ever do that again. The same goes for cussing."

Lily frowned. Boy was he mad. It didn't take much to rile him. She placed her hands on her hips and glared at him. "If I decide to cuss again, there ain't nothin' you can do about it!"

Ethan's expression darkened at her brazen retort, a flicker of something unreadable passing through his eyes. Placing a hand on her chin, he angled her face to his. "Don't test me, Lily," he warned, his voice tinged with a hint of warning. "I'll have you straight over my lap for a sound whopping, and believe me, I'm not a man to make idle threats."

"You can't do that!" she gasped. A thrill slipped unbidden through her slender body at the image he invoked, and annoyed with herself, she glared at him.

His eyes bore into her. "I can and I will."

"I'll tell my pa!"

"Would you like me to tell him you cussed? I can't see your pa letting you get away with that."

She looked at him mullishly. It was true. Her father would certainly punish her if he'd heard her cuss.

The tension crackled between them like lightning in a storm, a silent battle of wills unfolding. Turning her back on him, she spat. "I'm going back to the ranch."

"I'll come with you."

"Do what you like! I don't give a shi…" her eyes widened and she quickly amended her speech. "I don't care!"

· · ❧ · ·

Ethan laughed to himself as he watched her stalk over to her horse. His threat of a good bottom warming seemed to have worked. And he wouldn't hesitate either. One thing a woman should never do was cuss.

As they rode back to the ranch in tense silence, the frigid air seemed to mirror the chill that had settled between them. Twice he attempted to engage her in conversation, his voice gentle as he tried to break through her wall of stubborn silence, but she rebuffed him with a cold shoulder, her jaw set in defiance.

Ethan sighed inwardly, deciding to give up. She was a little firebrand, and with a spirit that independent, he knew it would take a while for her to mellow.

"Have it your own way, then," he muttered under his breath, resigning himself to the quiet ride back to the ranch. Luckily for him, solitude was something he was used to.

Upon their return to the ranch house, the tantalizing aroma of a homecooked meal greeted them. Ethan inhaled deeply and closed his eyes. If he wasn't mistaken, that was the fragrant scent of stew and fresh bread wafting through the air. His stomach growled in response.

Dismounting out the front, he led his horse into the stables and quickly settled her in. Lily did the same, still not saying a word to him or making eye contact. God she was one stubborn minx.

She stalked past him with her head held high and headed towards the kitchen, her steps purposeful and her expression unreadable. He followed closely behind, a silent presence in her wake. The desire to spank her sassy little backside as it swayed in front of him was almost overwhelming, but he willed self-control, knowing it would be inappropriate at this precise moment.

As they entered the cozy dining room, Lily's father looked up from his seat at the head of the table, his weathered face smiling at them. "Ah, there you both are. Just in time for lunch."

As he settled into his seat, her father asked him, "So Ethan, what do you think of our land?"

Ethan cleared his throat. "Your land is breathtaking, sir," he began, his tone sincere. "And from what I saw of the town, this is a fine place to live."

"Dispense with the 'sir'; just call me John."

"Of course."

He glanced at Lily and noticed her eyes flickered towards his for a brief moment, a glimmer of curiosity and something more passing through her gaze before she averted her eyes once more. She seemed to be thawing a little. It was about time.

Her mother came in with a big pot and put it in the middle of the table. As she took off the lid, a big cloud of steam rose up, and Ethan sniffed appreciatively. "That smells mighty good. I could smell it from outside."

Mary grinned at him. "Ma cooks lovely food, Mr. Blackwood."

Martha served Ethan first, placing a bowl of steaming food in front of him. "Help yourself to bread, Ethan. There's plenty to go around."

• • ⚜ • •

Halfway through the meal, Lily decided to tell her father about the Cougar. He looked surprised. "Must have been injured. We don't usually get them attack like that. That's worrying." He stroked his chin, deep in thought.

"I don't know, pa. It seemed alright, just angry as hell." *Just like Ethan*, she thought, glancing across the table.

"Well, thank the Lord you were there, Ethan." He remarked. "I don't think you should go out on your own, Lily. Not for a while. Just until we can make sure the varmint won't come back."

Lily rolled her eyes. "Pa, I can use a gun, you know! If Ethan hadn't been there, I'm sure I would've been able to fend the critter off."

Ethan settled his eyes on her. "I agree with your pa. You may be able to handle a gun, but the speed that animal moved was out of your league."

"Out of my league?" she bristled. "My aim is second to none. I could've killed that critter in a heartbeat."

"Now, now, Lily. Settle down. I'm sure Ethan's just worried about you, the same as we all are."

Lily gave a small huff and, scraping up the last of her food, finished her meal and stood up. "Come on, Mary, help me clear up, and we'll fetch dessert."

Martha smiled at her two daughters. "I made an apple and prune cobbler. It's on the kitchen table."

• • ⌘ • •

"**D**on't you worry none about Lily, Ethan." Martha said when the girls were out of earshot. "She's no milksop. She can take care of herself most of the time."

John quirked an eyebrow. "Not when there's an angry cougar about."

"But she's good with a gun, John." Martha insisted. "I think curtailing her independence will make her hard to live with. She's fiery enough at the best of times."

"She's not too old to get a good hiding if she does." John remarked, tapping his fingers on the table. He pointed his finger at his wife. "And don't think I won't."

Ethan nodded quietly. A man after his own heart. He'd been right when he mentioned to Lily that her father wouldn't like her cussing. He just knew it.

"I can always keep an eye on her whenever I'm outside," he offered. "And talking of the cougar, I reckon you might have to catch it or kill it if you see it again. Food's scarce in the snow. It could've been one of the reasons it was trying to hunt us."

"I reckon you're right." John agreed. "Keep a close eye on the surroundings when you're on the land."

"Will do."

Lily and Mary returned with the warm fruit cobbler, and the subject was dropped for now. But Ethan knew that little Miss Independent wasn't going to like having her movements monitored; that was a dead cert.

· · ❧ · ·

After lunch, Lily went to the barns to clean the stables. Mary was right behind her, dragging her feet.

"Oh, get a move on, Mary. The sooner you do it, the sooner you can do something else."

"Can't you do it?"

Lily stopped for a moment and turned around, her hands on her hips. "What? All this on my own? I don't think so, do you?" She glared at her sister. "In fact, why don't you do it all on your own?"

Mary pouted. "Well, that ain't fair."

"What's good for the goose is good for the gander." She raised an eyebrow.

"Eugh!" Mary flounced past her and headed into the stables. "Alright, I get the message."

"Good!"

They both picked up a shovel and began clearing out the old and replacing it with the new. Half way through, they paused for a break.

Lily wiped her face with a hanky. As cold as it was, she was still breaking out in a sweat. Her horse snickered at her, and she laughed. "Yes, your oats are coming. Just as soon as we've finished cleaning up your mess."

Mary stroked the chestnut mare's nose through the fence. "Feather's so greedy."

"She certainly is."

"Are you still taking her out this afternoon?"

"Of course."

"But what about Pa's rule to stay close to home?"

Lily sniggered, "What rule?"

"Are you gonna disobey Pa?" Mary gasped, her eyes wide. "If he finds out, he'll take his belt to you!"

"Well, then. I'd better make sure he damn well doesn't find out, and you, miss, ain't gonna say nothin' either!"

"If he asks me, I ain't gonna lie. I did that last time and got a thrashing for it." She looked at her and frowned. "Can't you just do as he asks?"

Lily shook her head. "No. I told Elspeth I was gonna meet her in town, and I ain't gonna let her down." She shot her sister a wicked grin. "Besides, she promised me some more of that moonshine."

"Lily!' Mary said, looking around to make sure no one else was around to hear her scandalous words. "You said you weren't gonna get anymore!"

"Well, I changed my mind. Anyway, don't worry about it. Let's finish our chores, then I can head off."

Mary picked up her shovel and, shooting her one last condemning look, said, "Well, don't expect any sympathy from me when Pa roasts your butt!"

Half an hour later, with the chore complete, Lily went indoors to get washed and changed into something decent to wear into town. Her parents were out visiting their neighbours, like they always did on a Tuesday, which left her the freedom she required to slip out unnoticed. Perfect.

With a determined glint in her eyes, she saddled her horse with swift, practiced movements, her heart pounding with a mix of excitement and apprehension. She knew she was disobeying her father, but she had no intention of him finding out. No, siree.

A few minutes later, she set off towards the horizon, the light wind tangling her blonde hair and the winter sun warming her back as she rode into the vast expanse of the countryside, the promise of freedom beckoning her forward.

Chapter Three

Ethan was hard at work in one of the fields; his mind focused on the task at hand—mending broken fences. As he paused to wipe the sweat from his brow, a flash of movement caught his eye in the distance. He frowned. It was a rider, and he immediately recognized that it was none other than Lily. And more to the point, she was on her own! Where in tarnation did she think she was going?

Without a moment's hesitation, Ethan mounted his horse with practiced ease, the powerful animal surging beneath him as he urged it into a gallop. The rhythmic beat of hooves thundered through the snow, carrying him swiftly towards her.

As he drew closer, his jaw set in a firm line as he prepared to confront her. The wind whipped through his dark hair, his eyes fixed on her figure as he closed the distance between them, determined to bring her back to safety.

Her father had already told him that he and Martha would be out that afternoon, and it seemed Lily had chosen the opportunity to sneak out. Little madam.

He called out to her. "Lily!"

He watched her turn around in the saddle, her eyes wide with shock, and then she urged her horse to go faster.

"Lily! Stop this minute!" He bellowed, but it made no difference.

Swearing under his breath and giving a determined kick to Nyx's flanks, he closed in on her.

He caught up to her within seconds. She glanced at him, her face angry. "Go away!"

"Rein in your horse. Now!" He ordered her.

"No!"

Before she had a chance to stop him, he leaned over and grabbed her reins, swiftly bringing both their mounts to a standstill, the powerful animals snorting and pawing at the ground as if mirroring the tension that crackled between the two riders.

"Lily, I don't know where you think you're going, but you need to turn back and head home." Ethan's voice was firm, his gaze locked on hers, leaving her in no doubt that he was serious. "You heard what your pa said."

He watched her emerald eyes spark with defiance as she attempted to slap his hand away from her reins, her frustration bubbling to the surface. "Let me go, Ethan," she demanded, her voice tinged with irritation. "I don't need you telling me what to do."

Ethan's jaw clenched at her resistance, his patience wearing thin. "Listen to me, Lily," his voice held a steely edge, a warning laced within his words. "You need to return home immediately. This isn't a game."

As the tension between them mounted, Lily's horse shifted beneath her, sensing the charged atmosphere that hung in the air. With a defiant glare, she attempted to rip the reins out of his hands and spur her mount forward, intent on escaping.

But Ethan's hand shot out with lightning speed, catching her wrist in a firm grip as he pulled her back towards him. "I won't ask you again, Lily," his voice held a note of finality, his eyes dark and intense as they bore into hers. "Return home now, or I'll be forced to tan your hide."

• • ❧ • •

As the tension between them reached a boiling point, Lily's eyes widened in disbelief at Ethan's stern resolve. "You can't be serious," she protested, her voice tinged with anger. "You can't just dictate what I do like this."

His firm grip on her wrists was doing funny things to her stomach. She glanced down, noticing how huge they were against her own. Lord, imagine having them big mitts on her little tush!

She met his eyes again. His expression remained steadfast, his gaze unwavering as he met her challenge head-on. "I'm dead serious, Lily," he stated firmly, his tone brooking no argument. "Your safety is my priority, and I won't stand by while you put yourself in harm's way."

A flicker of frustration crossed Lily's features, her jaw clenched in stubborn resistance. "Fine!" She relented begrudgingly, her gaze flashing with a hint of rebellion. "I won't go. You can let me free now."

Ethan's eyes narrowed, and after a couple of seconds, he released his grip on her. "I'll accompany you to make sure you get back safely," he offered, his tone softening slightly. "Let's head home, Lily."

But Lily had other ideas. If he was stupid enough to think she was going to obey him, then he was in for a surprise! She took the opportunity to urge her horse into a gallop

Without a second thought, Ethan reacted with swift decisiveness, his strong arms reaching out to grasp her and hoist her effortlessly from her horse onto his.

"Get off!" she gasped, scrabbling to hold onto the reins, but Ethan was way too big and strong to fight against. Her horse carried on without her a few feet and then stopped, immediately dropping its head to search around for some grass amongst the snow.

"Seems like you need a lesson, Lily."

"No, I don't!" She protested, struggling to break free.

Ethan dismounted, still holding her struggling form tight in his arms, and then manhandled her over to a fence. Raising one of his legs, he put his booted foot on the lower rung and threw her straight over his thigh.

Oh, Lord. He was actually going to spank her! What the heck!

"This isn't fair!" She wailed. "You'll regret it!"

"No, I won't, but you will." He said firmly.

With a resolute expression, Ethan threw her skirts over her back and, raising his hand, delivered a series of firm swats to her bloomer-clad backside, the sound echoing through the stillness of the countryside.

Lily wailed and kicked, but it made no difference. She had pushed him too far, and now she was reaping the consequences. As the sting of his discipline seared through her pride and stubbornness, Lily's protests turned to startled gasps, her cheeks flushing with embarrassment.

"Oh, it hurts! Can't you stop?"

"Uh-uh, little girl. Your behaviour has led to this. I won't be satisfied until you've learned your lesson."

His hand swung down again and again, the loud slaps filling the air around them. Lord, it was painful!

The weight of Ethan's authority bore down upon her, and she truly wished that she hadn't chosen to defy him! She had misjudged him in thinking that he wouldn't carry out his threat. Big mistake!

· · ⚘ · ·

Ethan held Lily tight against his side as he continued to rain down hard swats on her errant bottom. She was one of the most stubborn women he'd ever met.

He watched her slender legs kick up in the air, but it made no difference. She was far too petite against his strength and size. It served the little madam right. He thought about parting her bloomers and delivering her punishment on bare skin, but maybe it was a step too far. Her bloomers were only thin, and from the way she was wailing, his spanking was doing the job he intended.

"I hate you!" she spat, panting between smacks.

"Don't bother me, none, Lily. As long as you heed my words and don't break the rules, we'll get along fine."

"Oooh!" He heard her grit her teeth and smiled to himself. She was one stubborn little girl.

With a volley of hard smacks, he finally decided to bring her punishment to an end. Laying his hand flat over one buttock, he could feel the heat emanating through the thin fabric of her bloomers. Oh, yes. She'd have a very uncomfortable ride back, and it served her right.

Releasing his grip around her waist, he lowered his thigh, and she scrambled to stand up, clutching both hands on her sizzling bottom, her eyes glaring defiantly at him.

"You'd better take that look off your face right now, little girl, or I'll continue until you do!"

She opened her mouth to give him a sassy retort and then seemed to think better of it and lowered her eyes.

"Right, we're now going back to the ranch, and if you dare disobey your father again, I'll give you double what you just had. Understand?"

Her eyes flickered back to his, and he could see she was struggling with her emotions. The desire to badmouth him was strong; he could tell, but his desire to dominate her was equally so.

They stared at each other in a clash of wills, but finally she muttered a low, "Very well."

They rode back to the ranch in a heavy silence. The tension in the air was palpable, a tangible reminder of the swift discipline that had passed between them.

He noticed Lily shift uncomfortably in the saddle, and Ethan hoped it would be a nice little reminder of what happens to defiant little girls because, as sure as apples were apples, he wouldn't hesitate to do it again.

• • ❧ • •

The discomfort in her backside gnawed at Lily's pride. She hadn't ever been spanked by anyone other than her father before. She felt a sense of chastened humility mixed with a sudden desire for the large cowboy riding beside her.

She frowned. Why the hell would she feel desire for a man who'd just spanked her?

After a stretch of quiet contemplation, Lily's voice broke the stillness. "Ethan?"

"Mmm?" He said, his deep voice sending vibrations of pleasure washing over her. She mentally shook herself, annoyed that she felt anything towards someone who had just taken her to task.

"You won't tell my pa what happened, will you?"

He turned and looked at her, his expression thoughtful. For a moment she thought he wasn't going to agree, but finally, he nodded in quiet agreement, "I won't tell him. You've been punished enough, but hear me well, this cannot happen again."

She chewed her lip and looked away. For now, she would agree, but she really wanted to meet up with Elspeth, and one way or another, she would get there without any of them finding out. She was devious and cunning; she would come up with another way. She would make sure of it.

. . ৵৹ . .

That evening, around the dinner table, John asked him how he'd got on during the day. Ethan noted a flicker of alarm pass over Lily's face as her eyes shot to his. He leaned back in his chair and said easily, "I fixed a lot of the fencing on the east side. I'll start on the west side tomorrow."

"That's good. I know a lot of the posts need replacing. Perhaps we should go into town tomorrow and take the wagon. Load it up with new wood."

"Oh, can I come, pa?" Lily immediately chimed in.

"Course you can, Lily. As long as your ma doesn't need you here." He looked at Martha expectantly.

"No, you can go, Lily."

"She just wants to meet Elspeth." Mary interjected. Ethan noticed colour rise up in Lily's cheeks, and he wasn't sure if it was anger, embarrassment, or both, but she must have kicked her sister under the table because Mary suddenly let out a small yelp.

"Are you alright, Mary?" Her mother asked.

Mary reached down and rubbed her leg, her eyes shooting daggers at Lily. "Yes, I just knocked the table leg, that's all."

"Try to be more careful, dearest. What did you want to see Elspeth for, Lily?"

"Oh, nothing special. She just promised to give me a book. I haven't seen her for a while, so it'll be nice to have a bit of a catch-up."

"Is she a friend of yours?" Ethan asked her, his eyes sweeping over her tinged cheeks. She was hiding something that was for sure.

"Yes, her father owns the mercantile store you're going to."

He noted she busied herself with helping her mother serve out the dinner. She was refusing to meet his gaze, which told him she was most definitely hiding something. He decided to keep a close eye on her tomorrow. If she was up to no good, he was going to find out.

. . ❧ . .

The next afternoon, the weather turned a tad colder. Lily sat between the two men as her father steered the wagon towards town. She had a blanket wrapped around her for extra warmth and was mighty glad of it. She huddled between them, her head bowed as the icy wind stroked her cheeks.

"Lord, it's cold." She muttered.

Ethan looked at her sideways. "You can lean into me if you like."

A shiver of excitement rippled straight through her at the thought, but she was still mad at him for spanking her. Ain't no way she was going to lean into him.

"No, thank you; the blanket will warm me well enough."

His only response was a low chuckle under his breath, which immediately irked her. Great big galoot!

She shifted on the hard bench, trying to make her bottom more comfortable, but his spanking from yesterday was still making it throb. Why did he have to have such big, hard hands?

She glanced down at them resting on his knees. Clad in leather gloves, they looked even bigger. She ran her eyes up his sleeves, admiring his strength. As much as he annoyed her, she also knew she was attracted to him. He was dangerous, sexy, and didn't take any nonsense.

The clouds loomed heavy in the sky, casting a muted gray pall over the landscape as the wagon creaked along the rough hewn path. The rhythmic clatter of hooves mingled with the whistle of the wind as they made their way towards town. Ethan kept his gaze sharp and observant while her father gripped the reins. She admitted to herself that sitting between them, she felt quite safe, and maybe riding into town yesterday might have been a big mistake.

As they arrived in town and the wagon came to a halt outside the mercantile, Ethan's gaze flickered towards Lily as he climbed down off the bench seat. She immediately noticed and arched an eyebrow. "Why are you looking at me like that?"

"Just wondering if you wanted a hand getting down, that's all."

"Oh, I see."

She held her hand out, and ignoring it, he placed his big hands around her tiny waist and lifted her straight down onto the ground in front of him. She noticed his hands lingered a little, and she couldn't help the blush that stole over her cheeks at their close proximity.

She made a show of brushing down her skirts as he took his hands away—anything to avoid eye contact. He confused her. One minute she didn't like him, the next she felt a surge of desire. This wasn't at all like her. She was usually quite clear-headed and determined. Especially where men were concerned.

Her father appeared by her side and pulled a piece of paper out of his pocket. "Ma gave me a list of things to buy. You see to that, Lily, and we'll sort out the wood."

"Sure thing, pa." She took the list and followed behind the two men as they entered the mercantile store. She spied Elspeth straight away. She was serving Alice Clipford, a girl Lily wasn't that keen on. She talked too much. Way too much.

Leaving the men to talk to the owner, she quickly made her way over to Elspeth, who grinned happily on seeing her. Alice turned around and smiled when she saw her. "Good morning, Lily. I've nearly finished my purchases if you want to wait."

"Hello Alice. No, that's fine. I'll come back when you've finished. I just have to look at the err... ribbons. You carry on."

When Alice turned around, Lily winked at Elspeth and grinned before heading over to the other side of the shop. She really didn't fancy talking to Alice now or at any time really. Her incessant chattering usually gave her a headache.

She glanced at the various ribbons lying in neat coils on the haberdashery counter. She picked up a deep red velvet and held it up to the light. It would look so pretty for Christmas. But they didn't have much money for frivolities. Maybe she could ask her pa to get her one as a present for Christmas. She'd put in a big hint when they got home.

Reluctantly putting it down, she glanced over to see Alice leaving with a big box of shopping. She opened the door for her and then rushed over to Elspeth.

"Shall we go somewhere quiet?"

Elspeth called over to her father, "I'm just taking a quick pause, pa. Won't be long!" and grabbing Lily's hand, they almost ran to the door and exited the shop.

Lily didn't see the look that Ethan gave them. If she had, maybe she'd have been a bit more cautious...

Chapter Four

Seeing the mischievous glint that danced in Lily's emerald eyes was enough to tell Ethan that she was definitely up to no good.

He thought about saying something to her father but decided to deal with it himself. He could be wrong after all. But he had to find out.

With a sense of determination, he excused himself from the negotiations between John and the owner, telling them he'd be back shortly, and with purposeful steps, he made his way outside.

The girls weren't anywhere to be seen, but they couldn't have gone far. He walked along the boardwalk and then peered down the side of the building, spotting them immediately. They were engaged in a hushed conversation.

He stayed quietly watching them to try and ascertain what they were doing. Maybe it was just girls being girls. But then he reminded himself that Lily wasn't just any girl. She was a defiant, reckless little baggage. He kept in the shadows and studied them.

. . ⚜ . .

As Lily stood outside the mercantile store, the crisp air nipping at her cheeks, she shared a moment of laughter with Elspeth when she handed her a big bottle of moonshine.

"Oh, my, Elspeth!" she sniggered. "You weren't lying when you said it was big!"

The bottle of moonshine gleamed in the sunlight.

"Told you!" Elspeth declared smugly. "Ainsley stole it from mean ole Sam. He won't even notice he's got so much of it." She pulled a face. "Anyway, he's out of his mind on the stuff most days."

"Well, as long as Ainsley doesn't get into trouble. It's mighty fine of him to get it for us though."

Lily's eyes sparkled with mischief as she pulled the cork off the bottle and passed the bottle to Elspeth, a daring smile playing on her lips. "Go on, take the first mouthful!"

"What here? Now?" Elspeth said, her eyes wide.

"Why not? Ain't no one around." She had a brief look about her and, lost in the thrill of the moment, failed to notice the figure hidden in the shadows.

Elspeth raised the bottle to her lips and took a sip of the fiery brew, gasping as the liquid went down her throat. "Oh, Lord, that's so strong!"

Lily did the same and gasped herself. When she spoke, her voice was raspy. "Lord, that'll put hairs on your chest!"

Elspeth laughed loudly. "I don't want hairs on my chest; thank you very much!"

Lily took one more sip, enjoying the heady warm feeling it gave her as it slipped down a treat. Elspeth declined, saying, "I have to have a clear head for serving in the shop. I'll wait until I come over. Is Saturday still alright with you?"

"Sure. Although I can't promise there'll be any left by then."

"You greedy madam! Don't you dare drink it without me; else I'll take it back."

Lily held it close to her chest. "Uh-uh. This is mine!" She grinned devilishly and then laid a hand on her friend's sleeve. "I'm only kidding. No, I won't drink a drop until you come over. I promise!"

Putting the bottle in her small carpet bag, she linked her arm through Elspeth's and said, "Well, we'd better get my ma's shopping list sorted out before anyone notices anything amiss!"

Laughing, they walked back into the shop, both unaware of the storm brewing from their actions.

With all their shopping finished and the wood loaded up onto the wagon, Ethan offered to assist Lily up onto the wooden seat. He eyed the bag she held closely to her side, knowing full well what was in there.

"Shall I take that for you? I can put it in the back with the rest of the goods."

"No!" she said sharply and then quickly adjusted her tone. "I mean, no thank you. I'll keep it on my lap."

His eyes bore into hers, and she frowned, a look of unease coming over her face. His expression didn't change. He wanted her to know something was up.

He took her hand and helped her climb the step up to the seat. As she settled, he drew the blanket up over her and tucked it in either side, leaning close to her face. Again, he looked straight into her eyes, and he saw the flicker of uncertainty.

He sat down beside her, and her father flicked the reins to get the wagon moving towards home.

For a while they rode in silence until John said to Lily, "Did you get the book you wanted from Elspeth?"

"Oh, errr... no, she had one but it didn't interest me."

Ethan's lips thinned, listening to her lie to her father. A girl should never lie, especially to her parents. She had no intention of getting a book. No, this naughty little madam had something she shouldn't.

But that was going to be alright because he intended to take it off her just as soon as they returned home.

• • ❧ • •

Lily fidgeted on the ride back home. Something in Ethan's eyes made her uneasy. It was as though he knew what she had in her possession. But how? Unless he'd followed her and Elspeth earlier. But she hadn't seen him. No, it must be something else bothering him, but what?

She looked down at the bag she held tightly on her lap and risked a sideways glance at him. He raised an eyebrow and stared back solemnly. Oh, crikey. He must know. Damnation. How the heck had he found out?

The tension in the air was palpable as the wagon trundled along the familiar road towards home, and Lily kept quiet, trying to work out a plan of action as soon as she returned home. She needed a good hiding place for her moonshine. Somewhere, Ethan Blackwood would never find it in a million years!

The fading light cast long shadows across the landscape, and despite her blanket, Lily felt a sudden shiver ripple through her. That was when she spotted the cougar.

A gasp escaped her lips as the menacing figure stood in the middle of the path ahead, its golden eyes gleaming with feral intensity.

"Pa!" Lily whispered, pointing ahead. But her father and Ethan had already seen it.

Her father reined in the horses with a steady hand, the muscles in his jaw clenched with determination as he assessed the situation.

"Ethan." Her father's voice was a low rumble, laden with an unspoken urgency. "Take a hold of the reins."

Ethan immediately leaned across Lily and took control of the horses. They were already pawing the ground and trying to backup, naturally spooked by the threat right in front of them.

Picking up his rifle, her father took aim, but the cougar was quicker than lightning. With a flash of sinew and fur, it hurtled towards the lead horse with a primal ferocity that set the horses rearing up in their haste to escape the snarling animal.

Ethan tried to hold them steady, but the wagon began reeling sideways in a chaos of hooves and dust. Her father took aim as best he could as the beast reared up before them.

The crack of the gunshot echoed through the stillness of the wilderness, a sharp report that shattered the peace of the evening as the bullet found its mark between the cougar's eyes, felling the creature instantly. Thank God for her father's eagle-eyed marksmanship!

As the dust settled and the echoes of the gunshot faded into the twilight, Lily found herself clinging tightly onto Ethan's strong arms. He still had a tight hold on the horses reins, and they were already calm, a testament to his quick reflexes in the face of danger. She looked up into his eyes. Dang, they were sexy.

"Are you alright?" He asked, concerned.

She nodded and quickly withdrew her hands, a little embarrassed at the close proximity. "Yes, thank you."

"That was a clean shot, John." Ethan said, jumping down off the wagon. Her father followed suit, and they both stood over the dead animal.

"Such a fine creature." Her father said. "Sad to kill it, but we had no choice."

"No, you certainly didn't." Ethan agreed sadly, "What do you want to do with it?"

"Let's put it on the wagon and take it back. Give it a decent burial."

When the cougar was safely stashed in the back, Ethan walked around to look at the wagon wheels. "That was mighty lucky. I thought we might sustain some damage, but everything looks fine."

Her father laid a hand on one of the big wheels. "This wagon has seen many things, Ethan. It's part of the family." He grinned, patting the wood affectionately. "And like this family, it's strong. Ain't that right, Lily?"

• • ⌘ • •

Ethan's eyes locked with Lily's as she responded to her father. "Sure is, pa. Ain't no one ever put us down yet."

Ethan gave her a low, calculating smile. When he got hold of her moonshine he was going to tan her backside. Then they'd see how strong she was.

He noticed her smile falter slightly as she noted his direct look and flushing hotly, she looked away.

Oh, yes. She knew what was coming.

The ride back didn't take long. The cougar had attacked them on the perimeter of the Montgomery land, so the ranch came into view very quickly.

A steady plume of smoke billowed from the chimney, and Ethan could smell something delightful being cooked wafting across the path.

"Oh, smells like Martha's cooked something tasty for our dinner. But then she always does." John grinned, his eyes crinkling with happiness. "There's nothing nicer than having a woman cook you a welcoming meal."

A wave of sadness washed over Ethan as he remembered how Carrie used to cook. It had been pretty dire, but it hadn't mattered. She was all that mattered to him. He looked down, feeling slightly melancholy.

Suddenly, a little gloved hand settled over his, and he looked up in surprise to find Lily staring at him softly. Her emerald eyes stared into his, and for a moment time stood still, their souls locked in a moment of shared intimacy. She knew exactly how he felt.

The wagon jolting to a halt shook both of them back to the present, and Ethan quickly jumped down off the wagon, holding his hands out towards Lily. His large hands spanned her little waist, and he quickly lifted her down onto the ground.

They stared at each other for a moment before her father's voice broke the silence. "Take the horses into the barn, Ethan. We'll leave the wagon here to unload after dinner. I'm starving. Lily, go and tell your ma we'll be in shortly."

• • ❧ • •

Clutching her carpet bag, Lily did as her father bid and entered the house. The smell of freshly cooked bread reached her nostrils, and she sniffed appreciatively.

"I heard the wagon roll in. How did it go?" Her mother said, stirring a pot of gravy.

"Ma, you'll never guess, but Pa shot the cougar!"

Her eyes widened. "Oh, my! Is everyone alright? It didn't harm any of you?"

"Thankfully no. They've brought it back if you want to look."

Her mother pulled a face. "Not sure I want to." She glanced at Lily's bag. "Did you get the book you wanted?"

"No. Dang shame. Elspeth promised she'd have it for me next time, though." She turned around. "I'm just going to put my bag in the bedroom. I'll be back to help lay the table in a minute."

"Don't dawdle."

"Yes, ma." She rolled her eyes behind her mother's back and quickly ran up the stairs. Now where to hide her moonshine so no one could find it? Mary was a nosy little rascal, so it had to be somewhere good. Taking a chair, she dragged it over to her wardrobe and put the bag right at the back. Ain't no way Mary was going to look up there.

Grinning, she shoved the chair back in its place and ran downstairs to help lay the table.

The men came in and, after ditching their coats and gloves in the hallway, stood in front of the welcoming fire.

"Reckon it'll be a long winter." Her father said to Ethan. "Are you going somewhere for Yuletide, or will you remain here, because you're quite welcome to sit at our table. Martha always makes plenty of food. We usually invite the vicar and his wife."

"I would like that." Ethan replied.

Lily could tell by his tone that his words were genuine. She placed the knives and forks down, thinking about earlier on the wagon. She had felt his sadness and felt a need to comfort him. It seemed to have worked. Thinking of him being with them at Christmas gave her a warm fuzzy feeling, and she paused. Was she falling for him?

"Quit dithering, Lily." Her mother reprimanded her, "Hurry up or our dinner will get cold."

"Yes ma."

Halfway through lunch, Mary appeared, looking a little tired.

Her mother smiled at her. "Are you feeling better now, honey?"

"Yes, that lie down did me the world of good."

"Lie down?" Lily exclaimed, a frisson of alarm rushing through her. "I thought you were visiting Abigail."

Mary's eyes twinkled with devilment. "I thought you didn't notice me in the bedroom."

Lily's mouth went dry as dust. Oh, Lord. This wasn't good. She watched in horrified fascination as Mary drew her hands from around her back and held the bottle of moonshine up to her father.

"Pa, Lily put this on top of the wardrobe. I think it's moonshine."

Lily couldn't help the gasp that fell from her lips, and her cheeks went hot with alarm. The room fell silent, the only sound coming from the crackling fire as all eyes turned on Lily.

· · ∾◌∾ · ·

Watching the scene unfold, Ethan knew he had to do something. Lily was a naughty girl, but that was something he wanted to deal with in his own way.

"Ah, sorry, Lily. I forgot to take it off you." He threw his napkin down and stood up, striding confidently over to Mary and taking the offending bottle out of her hands. Her mouth made a little O of surprise.

"It's yours?"

"Indeed, it is. During all the commotion when your pa shot the cougar, I gave it to Lily for safekeeping." He knew this line would be a great distraction. "Did you know we shot a cougar today?"

"No!" She gasped. "Was it that nasty one that's been prowling around?"

"The one and the same. Your pa here is a skilled shooter. That varmint didn't stand a chance."

"Pa! Tell me what happened." Mary immediately rushed over and took a seat next to her father. "Was it big? Did it growl? Did it threaten you?"

Whilst she was talking, Ethan sat back down and darted a glance at Lily. Her eyes were wide, and her cheeks were bright red. He saw her swallow hard, and she shot him a look of silent thanks. What she didn't know was that she was going to get a good bottom warming as soon as he got the chance.

She had behaved badly, and he felt it only right that he dish out the right punishment on her peachy little backside.

Chapter Five

Lily's heart had leapt into her throat when her conniving younger sister dared to reveal she had moonshine. Obviously she wanted to get her into trouble. Little mischief maker!

Well, two could play at that game.

First of all, she had to deal with Ethan Blackwood. Even though he'd come to her rescue, she had a feeling it was going to come with consequences. After all, nothing in life was free.

And would he give her the moonshine back? She highly doubted it. Not if the look on his face was anything to go by. In fact, his look spoke volumes, and she reckoned he might just turn her over his knee again for another spanking. It sent a tremour of excitement and fear rippling straight through her.

Her small white teeth chewed on her bottom lip as she tried to get her emotions under control. She had no idea why the thought of going over his knees was so exciting. I mean, it hurt. So why did the thought not alarm her as much as it should? In fact, her nether regions felt quite damp. Oh, Lord. Perhaps she should pray extra hard tonight for redemption. She was a naughty sinner for even thinking such thoughts.

After explaining to Mary how they'd shot the cougar and why, her father turned his attention onto Ethan and the bottle of moonshine on the table.

"I don't mean to lecture you on what you drink, Ethan, but that there moonshine is illegal."

"I know, and I do apologise for getting Lily involved. But, like I said, the circumstances earlier were rather unusual."

"Oh, of course." Her father agreed. "But to be perfectly truthful, Ethan, I'd rather you didn't have that on the premises."

His meaning was clear, and Ethan nodded quickly. "Absolutely. I didn't know that's how you felt. I'll go and get rid of it now."

Lily watched him pick up her bottle of moonshine and head for the door. Oh no! Her liquor!

. . ❧ . .

Shrugging his coat on, Ethan declined dessert and headed off to his log cabin, the offending moonshine bottle hanging in his hands.

The trouble that little girl caused!

When he reached the front door, he felt a tug on his sleeve and, looking down, found the defiant little blonde right by his side.

"Can we talk?" She asked tentatively.

Without a word, he inserted the key in the lock and opened the door, standing aside so she could enter first. She quickly nipped inside, and he followed.

He took off his coat and stamped his feet to get rid of the snow, and then kicked off his leather boots, waiting for her to do the same. She quickly drew them off and looked even smaller. Then he helped her off with her coat. Hanging it on the stand next to his.

"Come inside the living room. The fire's still crackling." He said, his voice low.

He placed the bottle of moonshine on the little table and sat down in one of the easy chairs, watching Lily as she paced nervously in front of him.

"I first of all want to say thanks for saving me back there. Pa would have been madder than a march hare if he knew that bottle was mine."

"Uh-huh," he agreed.

Her emerald eyes darted a glance at him, and then she paced some more. "But it's not as bad as you think. I was just holding that bottle for a friend of mine. He-he likes a drink now and then, so I help out. I know that sounds bad..."

"Yes, it does."

She faltered a little at his tone. She was clearly lying, but it would be interesting to see where this went. So he waited, silently, to see how big a hole she was going to dig for herself.

"So, I was wondering if you would see fit to give it back to me. You know, without informing Pa."

He waited a moment to see if there was any more to her tale and then slapped his thigh and gave a loud guffaw.

"Brilliant! Why, Lily, you should be on the stage!"

He watched her eyes narrow with anger, and she put her hands on her hips angrily whilst glaring at him. "What?"

"You heard me. You put on such a good show; you should share it with everyone."

"It's not a show."

"It is. You and I both know that you got that moonshine off Elspeth. It wasn't meant for anyone else but you two. Don't try and fool me otherwise."

• • ✿ • •

Hearing Ethan's words sent a surge of adrenaline running through her veins, a flush of fear and defiance rushing through her as she met his steady gaze.

In that moment, faced with the choice of defiance or submission, Lily opted for defiance. It was in her nature.

She glanced at the bottle on the table and decided she had only one option. Snatch it up and run! Closing her hand around the bottle, she picked it up and headed for the door, her head held high with determination.

He reached her in a heartbeat. "And where do you think you're going with that?"

"It's mine. Ain't for you to worry about where I'm going!"

He grabbed her shoulder and moved her over to the wall, putting one large hand above her head and peering right down into her face. "Maybe you should rethink your attitude, little girl."

She bit her lip, her breath coming in short rasps as her body responded to the obvious danger. She also felt moisture gather between her thighs unbidden, at such close proximity to the giant of a man. He smelled really good as well. Leather, wood smoke, and, of course, that cologne. Lord, give her strength!

Her eyes fell to his lips, so close to hers, and she swallowed hard, trying to control the surge of desire that ripped through her. She raised her eyes to his again, to find the hazel depths had turned a shade darker. Was he just angry, or did he feel as aroused as she was?

She felt him take the moonshine from her grasp.

"That's mine!" She protested, her bottom lip pouting and her eyes narrowing, watching helplessly as he put the bottle by the wall.

"Are you really going to keep this up?" He said, his eyes settling on her mouth. He placed his hand on her jaw and angled her face to his, his look intense.

Her lips parted softly, and she said, "Maybe." It came out as more of a whisper, her speech seeming to disappear at his touch. It was electric, and all she could focus on was his mouth as it descended over hers.

She made no move to stop him. She wanted him to kiss her. Plain and simple.

His lips were firm yet tender as he coaxed her into submission. Demanding and persuasive. She opened her mouth, moaning softly when his tongue slid inside her warm depths. She had never been kissed so thoroughly before, and her body responded willingly, surrendering to his masterful touch.

Her hands crept up his broad chest to settle on his shoulders while she felt his hands move to her waist, drawing her against his hard, masculine form. He was so big and powerful.

With his strong arms wrapped around her, she felt she would never come to harm.

They broke apart, and he looked down at her. "What am I going to do with you, Lily Montgomery?"

She gave him a slow smile. "You mean, what am I going to do with you, Ethan Blackwood?" She replied sassily.

He grinned, and taking her arm, he drew her over to one of the chairs. Taking a seat, he pulled her down onto his lap, wrapping his big arms around her waist. She regarded him steadily, her eyes sparkling. "Perhaps you should kiss me again?"

• • ❧ • •

"Oh, I intend to, just as soon as I've smacked your bottom." She gasped and tried to rise up, but he stopped her. "Did you think I wouldn't punish you?"

He watched her brow furrow as realisation dawned that she was in for a spanking. Maybe she thought all was forgiven because they had kissed. But uh-uh. He'd taken the blame for her illegal moonshine, so her little butt was in for a roasting. It was only fair, and after all, he was a fair man.

He watched the multitude of emotions wash over her face as she tried to think of a way out of her predicament, and placing a hand on her chin, he raised her face to his. "You know you deserve this, and you'll feel so much better after. I promise."

Her eyes widened, and she sputtered, "Better? How in tarnation will I feel better?"

He lifted her off his lap whilst still speaking to her. "Because, little girl, you know what you did was wrong, and you have two choices." He stood her in front of him, holding both her hands. "You can either take a bare bottom spanking or you can confess to your pa."

Her mouth made a small O of surprise. "But I can't tell, pa!"

"Well then." He sat back in the chair and patted his lap. "Over you go."

She pursed her perfect little lips and folded her arms over her chest. "But I don't want to do either. Ain't there no third choice?"

He shook his head and just stared at her, waiting quietly for her to accept her punishment.

She rolled her eyes and, huffing loudly, positioned herself by his side. Her eyes flashing daggers at him, she huffed, "You're being unreasonable."

"No, Lily, I'm not, and you know full well that's the plain truth. Now lean over." He pulled her over his lap and pushed her forward so her feet were off the ground and her hands were on the floor. "That's it."

Reaching for the hem of her dress, he drew the fabric over her back and then parted her bloomers. Her plump little bottom was soon revealed to his appreciative gaze. The perfectly smooth flesh was ripe for a good spanking.

. . ❧ . .

Lily closed her eyes, resigning herself to her fate. How the hell had she found herself in this position yet again?

I mean, why couldn't he just let her have the moonshine back? Why was he so unreasonable?

She felt his hand on her bare flesh and despite the realisation that her bottom was soon going to be on the receiving end of his large hands, she couldn't help the frisson of desire that rippled straight through her.

He moved a hand around her waist, hugging her to his side, so she couldn't move. Lord, this was going to hurt.

The first smack made contact with her delicate flesh, and she felt the sting immediately. She gritted her teeth and tried to remain quiet, not wanting to give him any satisfaction that it was hurting her. But as he carried on, swatting each cheek in a steady rhythm, she found that she simply couldn't refrain from voicing her pain.

"*Ouch! Oh!* That hurts!"

"Good! It's supposed to." He said, his deep voice sending shivers down her spine. "Bad girls get punished, Lily."

His large hand impacted on both cheeks at once, and she yelped. But it didn't stop him none. He just carried on, his hand swinging down again and again until her backside felt like a furnace. Lily narrowed her eyes angrily. She'd bet her last dollar he was enjoying this! Great galoot!

"*Aow!*" She wailed as he delivered a smack to her sit spots. "*Oooh!*"

With one last volley of swats, he finally stopped but kept her pinned in the same position.

"So, little girl, I want your truthful promise that you'll never get involved with illegal moonshine again? Not one drop shall pass your lips? Understand?"

She pulled a face and grumbled under her breath. Did he truly think she'd abide by his terms? Seriously?

He gave her a hard slap, the sound echoing around the little cabin. "Answer me, Lily."

"Yes, yes, alright." She hissed. The sting was intense. She'd agree to anything at the moment, but he didn't know her too well. If she wanted something, she'd do it anyway. Regardless. She'd just make damn sure he wasn't in the vicinity!

She felt his fingers pull her bloomers back together, and then he pulled her skirts back down over her tender bottom, finally releasing his hold on her.

She sprang up and rubbed her bottom furiously whilst glaring at him. She opened her mouth to speak, and he simply raised an eyebrow in warning, so she quickly looked away. Dang it. Tyrant.

She wasn't going to sit comfortably for days now because of his great mitts.

She turned around with the intention to leave, her eyes glancing over to the bottle of moonshine by the wall. So near yet so far.

Suddenly she found herself tumbling straight into Ethan's lap as he grabbed her wrist and pulled her down.

"Ethan!"

"I do believe you promised me a kiss."

Her bottom lip pouted sulkily, and she breathed, "That was before you blistered my backside."

He gave her a low, easy smile, instantly sending ripples of desire streaking through her. "But don't you feel better for it?"

"Nope," she said mullishly.

He laughed and cuddled her close against him, so her head was lying against his chest. She briefly thought about protesting but then decided that she kind of liked sitting on his large lap, even if he was a great big tyrant. It felt good to be held so close, especially to a man that set her nether regions on fire. She could hear his heartbeat through his shirt; the steady beat was quite comforting.

He placed his hand on her chin and angled her face up to his, his thumb rubbing over her bottom lip. "Has anyone ever told you how pretty you are, Lily?"

She blushed. "Maybe once or twice."

He smiled, setting her heart on fire and lowering his lips; he captured hers in a searing kiss. She sighed as a wave of pleasure washed over her. He sure knew how to kiss.

She placed her hands behind his neck, her fingers entwining in his dark brown hair as the kiss deepened. He slid his tongue into her mouth, and she couldn't help the small moan of desire that escaped her lips. It felt so good.

Even though her bottom was throbbing against his lap, it gave an extra sensation to the experience that she'd never felt before. Maybe Ethan was right. Maybe she did feel better after a spanking?

A few moments later, they broke apart, both a little breathless, but the spark that had been ignited between them was palpable.

"I'd better go back. Ma will be wondering where I am." She said softly.

He nodded and helped her rise up off his lap. "Now you've been punished for your sins, Lily; you can atone for them by taking that bottle of moonshine and pouring the contents on the ground outside." He walked over and picked up the bottle.

Lily's eyes lit up, and she crossed her fingers behind her back. "Of course. I'll take it home and empty it out the back."

No way was she going to do that. Once that bottle was in her grasp again, it was staying there! She saw Ethan give a wry smile as he replied, "We'll do it right now, outside. Come on."

She tried to hide the look of dismay on her face but failed, and as she joined him, he swatted her on her bottom.

She yelped and placed her hand over the offending sting. "What was that for?"

"You know exactly what that was for. Don't ever try and hoodwink me, Lily. It won't work." He held his hand out for her to take, and huffing a little, she placed her little hand in his. "Now, we'll do this together. That way, both of us can rest easy tonight."

"I won't." Lily grumbled as he walked her to the door. "My backside's on fire."

He didn't bother responding but simply shot her a look of reproach. Reaching for her coat, he helped her shrug it on before donning his own. Once their boots were on, they stepped out into the crisp night air.

Ethan watched her remove the lid from the bottle, and Lily sadly poured the contents onto the snowy ground, watching the last drops ebb away.

"Come on, little girl," Ethan smiled. "I'll walk you back."

He left her at the kitchen door, and she entered the house. Her mother and father were still up, sitting by the warm crackling fire.

"Were you keeping Ethan company?" Her mother asked, her eyes curious.

"Yes, I was telling him about the town and, you know, things to do over Yuletide."

"It'll be nice to have him here for Christmas. I hope he enjoys it."

"I'm sure he will. It's always a lovely atmosphere in Whispering Pines."

Perhaps she'd be able to kiss him under the mistletoe as well, she thought to herself, blushing. As she kissed her parents good night and made her way to her bedroom, she failed to see the knowing look they exchanged and the smiles that followed.

Chapter Six

C hristmas..

On a crisp December morning, the air was filled with the scent of pine and the sound of joyous laughter as Mary woke Lily up by jumping all over her bed.

"Wake up, Lily! It's Christmas!"

Lily groaned and drew the covers up over her head. "What time is it?"

"Six o'clock!"

"Six! Eugh! Let me sleep a little longer."

"No!" Mary said, flattening herself on top of her covers and making herself a dead weight to irritate her. "I ain't getting off until you get up!"

Lily growled and quickly leapt up, wrapping Mary in the covers so she was imprisoned, all the while laughing and tickling her. "Don't threaten me, you little rascal!"

A few minutes later, both breathless, they lay on the bed, side by side, breathing heavily and smiling.

There was nothing Lily liked more than Christmas. It was the day the Montgomery family gathered together and let their hair down. Of course, chores still had to be done, but that was life living on a ranch.

Lily felt her heart flutter with the magic of the season and also the knowledge that Ethan was with them this year. The last couple of weeks since the moonshine incident, they'd stolen kisses whenever they had the opportunity, and Lily knew her heart belonged to him.

They hadn't told anyone yet about their blossoming relationship, although she had a feeling her mother knew. Her mother never missed a thing!

Mary grabbed her hand. "Come on, let's get dressed for church. I'm going to wear my pretty blue dress. You should wear that tartan one Elspeth gave you."

"Good idea."

They both got dressed in record time and helped each other style their hair, leaving most of it hanging loosely over their shoulders and the sides pinned up with little flower clips.

"There, I think we'll do, don't you?" Lily grinned.

As Mary opened the door, she sniffed the air and smiled. "Ma's made pancakes!"

Lily's stomach growled in response, and she quickly followed Mary down into the kitchen.

She blushed furiously when she found Ethan already seated at the table, looking more handsome than ever in a smart waistcoat, crisp shirt, and bootlace tie. He was tucking into a pancake already, and by the look on his face, he was thoroughly enjoying it.

"Good morning, girls." Their mother said, "Merry Christmas."

"Merry Christmas, ma, and to you, Mr. Blackwood." Mary said, settling herself opposite him.

"Merry Christmas, Mary." He smiled and then looked at Lily. "And to you, Lily. You're both looking beautiful today, if I may say."

"Are you coming to church with us, Mr. Blackwood?" Mary asked him.

"I sure am." He leaned back and reached inside his waistcoat, bringing out two small parcels. He handed one to Mary and one to Lily. "I got a small gift for you both."

"Oh!" Mary gasped, her eyes wide. "I love presents."

Lily smiled, and her eyes twinkling with excitement, she accepted hers, opening the small, neatly wrapped parcel to find the very ribbon she'd been looking at in the mercantile store.

"Oh! It's beautiful," she breathed, stroking the dark red velvet.

"I saw you looking at it, so I figured it would make a good present."

"I love it!"

Mary had received a pretty blue ribbon. "Oh, it matches my dress, Mr. Blackwood! Thank you so much."

Their mother placed a plate in front of them with two pancakes on. "Honey's there if you want it."

"Where's pa?" Mary asked.

"He's getting the horses hitched to the wagon, ready to go to church. He'll be in soon." She placed her hands on her hips and smiled. "Now tuck in, then we can get going!"

Half an hour later, the family arrived at the little church in town. Nearly everyone was present, and there was a feeling of gaiety in the air.

Ethan helped Lily down off the wagon and let his hand linger on hers. "That ribbon really suits you, Lily. You look beautiful."

"Thank you for buying it, Ethan. I truly love it." Not only did she love it, but she loved him even more for noticing that she liked it in the first place.

$$\cdot \; \cdot \; \text{✧} \; \cdot \; \cdot$$

As the church bells rang out, signaling the end of the Christmas service, Ethan felt a sense of warmth and contentment wash over him that he hadn't felt in years. The glow of candlelight and the sound of carols had filled him with a sense of peace and joy, a feeling that only grew as he watched Lily laugh with her sister.

The red ribbon he'd given her was perched at the back of her head, woven into her fine golden strands of hair, and she looked beautiful. Stunningly beautiful.

He hadn't felt this way about a woman since his wife had died, and in all truth, maybe his love for Lily was stronger. They had a rare connection. Something deep and unspoken.

As she went to walk past him, he caught her arm gently. "Lily," his voice was low. "Can we talk? There's something I need to ask you."

Her eyes widened a little. "Of course."

He followed her outside the small church and, taking her hand, led her over to a large tree for privacy. As they stood beneath the boughs, she tilted her head as she waited for him to speak, her intelligent eyes keenly assessing him. No doubt trying to preempt what he was going to say.

He hid a smile and said, "Lily, I know we've only known each other for a short time, but I've come to realise that you mean a hell of a lot to me."

His words were heartfelt, his eyes searching hers for a glimpse of the love he held in his heart. "Will you marry me?"

The question hung in the air as her pretty emerald eyes stared up at him. For a moment he was unsure of her decision, but then she grinned and said, "Oh, Ethan." Her voice was a soft sigh, her eyes glistening with unshed tears of happiness. "Yes, a thousand times yes. I feel exactly the same."

He grabbed her to him, enveloping her slender form in his big, muscular arms. Over her head, he saw her father nod happily as he looked over at them. Ethan had already asked permission that very morning if he could wed his daughter, and he had agreed.

So all that needed to be done now was to inform everyone else.

• • ❧ • •

As her family settled in for their Christmas feast, the table groaned under the weight of hearty dishes and delectable treats that her mother had so painstakingly prepared. The crackling fire cast a warm glow across the room, illuminating the faces of her loved ones, including her soon-to-be husband, Ethan Blackwood.

Her father had already told her that they would build a separate ranch for them on the land so they could be independent. It would take a while, and for now, they could live in the cabin. She quite liked the idea of that. It was small and cozy. Plenty of room for her and Ethan.

She watched as Ethan stood up, raising his glass to her father. "John, I want to thank you for welcoming me into your home and your family."

Ethan's voice was sincere. "I know I haven't been here for very long, but I care deeply for your daughter, Lily, and I promise to always honour and protect her."

Her father's gaze softened at Ethan's words, a silent understanding passing between them as they shared a moment of unspoken respect. He nodded slowly and said in response, "Ethan, I appreciate your honesty, and I know you and Lily will get along just fine." He raised his glass, "and I welcome you as part of our family."

"Amen to that." Her mother said. "Now, help yourself, everyone. There's plenty to go around, and it's time to celebrate!"

. . ᘓ . .

After the meal and several games of cards, Ethan decided he needed some alone time with his wife-to-be. Her lips were just begging to be kissed, and he couldn't wait any longer.

Escorting her to his cabin, he helped her off with her shawl, and whilst she took her boots off, he shrugged off his own jacket and boots.

The next thing he gathered her straight into his arms and kissed her soundly. When they broke apart, he smiled down at her cute little face.

"I've been wanting to do that for hours."

"Me too!" Lily grinned.

Placing his hands on her tiny waist, he lifted her straight up into his arms and strode into the living area. Taking a seat, he settled her on his lap and once again laid claim to her delectable lips. She sighed and opened her mouth for him, her hands creeping up his chest to lace together at the back of his neck.

She tasted of sugar and spice, his little Christmas treat. His tongue fenced with hers, and she responded fervently, proving to be a fiery little temptress. That was the reason he'd fallen in love with her. That and her cute little butt.

He finally pulled away and looked deep into her eyes. "Merry Christmas, little girl. You have made me the happiest of men today."

She grinned wickedly. "So, when we get married, does that mean you won't have to spank me again?" She played with one of his shirt buttons. "I mean, men shouldn't have to spank their wives, should they?"

He grabbed her hand in his and looked her deep in the eyes. "If you behave, then there'll be no punishment. But can you promise to behave, little girl?" He reached down and cupped one of her pert little butt cheeks. "Or will I have to spank that naughty little bottom of yours?"

She drew in her bottom lip with her teeth and flashed him a cheeky look. "Well, in all honesty, Ethan, I just don't know."

He laughed and captured her lips again. She was a little madam, but he was sure gonna enjoy taming her!

The new year couldn't come soon enough, and then this sassy little baggage would be his wife. To have, to hold, and to spank when needed!

The end

If you liked this cowboy book - how about The Anderson Brothers?
This is a teaser from Book I: Brodie & Carrie Anne
https://a.co/d/88gKEqQ

Prologue

Iron Creek, Wyoming, 1878

The sun hung low in the sky, casting its golden glow over the rather dilapidated wooden facade of the house called Willow Ranch. The air was still, save for the faint rustling of the tall grasses that surrounded the property. Twenty-one-year old Carrie Anne Brown stood on the porch, her heart racing as she held a rifle in her trembling hands. She had never fired a gun in her life, but she wasn't about to let the man standing outside the ranch know that.

"Go on, you heard me, get out of here!" She shouted, her voice firm despite the uncertainty coursing through her. "You ain't got no business on this land."

The man didn't flinch. He stood there, calm and unmoving, his broad shoulders framed by the fiery hues of the setting sun. His arms hung loosely at his sides, though Carrie Anne could tell by the way he carried himself that he wasn't someone to be trifled with. He exuded confidence, the kind that came from years of hard living on the frontier.

He raised an eyebrow, his lips twitching, seemingly amused by the sight of her standing there with the rifle aimed squarely at him. Why wasn't he scared, dammit?

"I suggest you lower that rifle," he said, his deep voice carrying easily across the yard. "Before I have reason to blister your behind, young woman."

Carrie Anne's jaw dropped, and she gasped, her grip tightening on the rifle. "How dare you threaten me!" she snapped, her cheeks burning with indignation.

"It ain't a threat," the man replied evenly. "It's a warning. Now put that thing down before you hurt yourself."

His hazel eyes locked onto hers, and for a moment, Carrie Anne was struck by the sheer force of his gaze. They were the kind of eyes that seemed to pierce straight through to her soul, warm and golden with specks of green, yet unyielding and resolute. His features were ruggedly handsome. He had a strong jawline, a day's growth of stubble, and mid-brown wavy hair streaked with blonde highlights. He was tall and muscular, his broad chest and thick arms evident even beneath his checked shirt.

Her hands trembled as she tried to keep the rifle steady. She knew she was out of her depth, but pride wouldn't let her back down. She had to protect herself and her sister, no matter what. She tilted her chin up defiantly, her fiery nature taking over.

"I'll put it down when you leave!" She said, her voice quavering slightly despite her best efforts.

The man didn't move. He simply stood there, arms now crossed over his chest, his expression calm and unbothered. "I reckon you don't know what you're doin' with that thing," he said, nodding toward the rifle. "You're gonna end up shootin' yourself in the foot, or worse, me. And I don't take kindly to bein' shot at."

"I know exactly what I'm doin'," Carrie Anne lied, her cheeks flushing. The truth was, she'd never even held a rifle until about five minutes ago, when she'd picked it up from inside the kitchen. But she wasn't about to let him call her bluff.

"Is that so?" He said, his lips curving into a faint smirk. "Then why are your hands shakin'?"

Carrie Anne's breath caught, and she instinctively glanced down at her trembling hands. She cursed herself for the slip, but when she looked back up, the man's expression had softened slightly.

"Look, Miss..." He paused, waiting for her to supply her name.

"Brown," she said reluctantly. "Carrie Anne Brown."

"Miss Brown," he said with a nod. "I'm not here to cause trouble. I just need to talk to Dwight. I ain't no threat. But if you're still fixin' to shoot that rifle, you'd best know how to use it first."

Carrie Anne narrowed her eyes at him, refusing to let her guard down. "I can use it just fine! And just who are you, anyway?"

The man's smirk returned, though it was more good-natured this time. "Name's Brodie. Brodie Anderson." He raised his hand and pointed to the west. "My ranch is over yonder."

She tightened her grip on the rifle, determined not to let her unease show. "Well, Mr. Anderson," she said firmly, "you're trespassing on private property. And I'd appreciate it if you'd kindly leave."

Brodie sighed and shook his head, as if he found her stubbornness both amusing and exasperating. "You're a feisty little madam, ain't you?" he said. "But you're also out here in the middle of nowhere, alone, and pointin' a gun at someone who's twice your size. That ain't exactly the smartest thing to do."

Carrie Anne bristled at his condescending tone. "I'm not alone," she shot back. "But that ain't none of your business."

Brodie raised an eyebrow, clearly unconvinced. "That so?" He took his Stetson off for a moment and ran a hand through his hair before settling it back on again. "Miss Brown," he said patiently, "I ain't here to hurt you. Just tell Dwight that I called round, and I'll do so again tomorrow."

And with that, he turned and began walking back toward his horse, a sleek black stallion that stood grazing near the edge of the property. Carrie Anne watched him go, her emotions all jumbled.

As Brodie mounted his horse and tipped his hat to her, she found herself wondering just who this man was—and why his presence left her feeling so unsettled.

And that was how Carrie Anne Brown first got to meet Brodie Anderson.

. . ❧ . .

The other two books in the series will be:
Book II: Luke & Bonnie, Book III: Adam & Ellie Mae

. . ❧ . .

Fancy another teaser? You do? Okay... here's the beginning of A Passion for Annie!
https://books2read.com/u/mgev5x

Chapter One

1879 *Wyoming*
The cold winter winds whipped across the Wyoming plains as Annie Johnson helped her father finish the evening chores on their small homestead. Though she was only twenty-three, she had taken on much of the responsibility of running the farm since her mother had passed the previous year. It had been hard, but she knew her mother would be just as proud of her as her father was. Together they had overcome grief and learned to carry on.

As she brushed down their lone milk cow, Beth, her thoughts drifted to the coming Christmas holiday. Money had been tight lately, and she wasn't sure what she could do to make the season easier for her father. She needed to do something to take both their minds off the memory of losing her mother.

It had been in the depths of winter that she had taken her last breath. She would never forget it. Even a year later, it was still a fresh memory.

Finishing up, she patted Beth on the neck and said softly. "You don't care, do you, girl? As long as you get your food, nothing really matters, does it?"

Beth eyed her sideways, her big tongue coming out to lick her lips and uttering a low moan before tucking back into the pile of hay.

"You see, you knew I was talking about food." Annie laughed. She turned around and threw the brush in an empty bucket, and slipping out of the pen, she closed the gate behind her. Beth was known to be a bit of an escape artist, and Annie had learned to take no chances.

Her father was fixing some fences in the far field, his figure just visible beyond the barn. He worked hard to keep their smallholding running efficiently, and she appreciated it. Unlike her friend Amy's father, who just sat around drinking and dishing out orders to her and her brother.

She pursed her lips. She disliked the man intensely. The best thing Amy could do was get married and leave home. But decent, law-abiding eligible men around these parts were scarce, so Amy just kept her head down and carried on.

Much like her own journey in life. She longed to find a husband, yet the thought of leaving her father weighed heavily on her heart. She knew he could never manage this place alone. Perhaps if she found a man willing to share their lives and help run the homestead, it could work. But for now, that remained a distant dream.

"Well, this won't do, Annie Johnson!" She tutted under her breath. "Dinner won't make itself."

She walked over to the water pump and began to draw some water into a bucket so she could wash her hands. Picking up the small bar of coarse soap, she rubbed it on her hands and wiped the day's grime away. The water was so cold that her hands began to turn red. Washing the suds off, she reached into her coat for a cloth and quickly dried them.

"Dang, it's so perishing cold." She grumbled, brushing her blonde hair off her face.

Just then, a rider came over the hill. She frowned, trying to make out who it was. They weren't expecting anyone, as far as she knew.

She waited patiently for the rider to approach near enough so she could identify them. It was a big horse, and the man astride it was equally as big. He was riding with ease, his long legs gripping the horse's flanks and urging it forwards towards her.

A few moments later, she recognised who it was—Jed Wheeler, the most prosperous farmer in the valley. But the look on his face said this wasn't a social call. He seemed very serious.

He was quite a bit older than her, mid-thirties or thereabouts, and on the few occasions their paths had crossed, she'd always found him a little intimidating. He was a handsome man, with shoulder-length dark-brown hair and piercing hazel eyes. He stood at least a foot taller than her and then some.

His eyes met hers as he reined in his horse. "Is your pa home?" he asked gruffly.

She nodded, apprehension building in her stomach. What did he want with her father? "He's in the far field, over there." She pointed her finger in the distance, and Jed turned his head to look. Without another word, he turned his horse and rode off to see him.

She watched him for a moment. Her gut felt uneasy. Something wasn't right. It wasn't just his tone but the look in his eyes. She nibbled on a fingernail, wondering whether she should go over and listen in but then decided against it. Dinner had to be done. They were having stew, and she just needed to add some more vegetables to finish it off. The meat had already been cooking for a couple of hours, so it should be tender by now.

Reluctantly, she drew her gaze away and headed towards the house.

. . ❧ . .

Jed rode towards Abel Johnson with a determined mindset. He didn't like what he was going to say, but it had to be said.

He saw Abel's eyes flicker with concern as the noise of his horse alerted him to his presence. Jed dismounted, tilting his hat back, and walked over to him.

"Abel."

"Afternoon, Jed, what can I do for yuh?" Abel asked him cautiously. Jed could see in his eyes that he knew very well why he was there.

Jed cut straight to the point. "Your loan's six months overdue. I'm here to collect—one way or another."

"Has it been six months already?" Abel breathed, trying to stall. "I-I didn't realise it'd been so long, Jed. Truly, I didn't."

Jed quirked an eyebrow. "Abel, I sent you two letters; don't tell me you never received either of them."

"Well, I mean to say, I think I did receive one, but that was a while back and..."

"Do you have the means to pay me or not?" Jed asked, cutting to the chase. He wasn't a patient man at the best of times, and Abel's obvious attempt to forestall him was starting to grate.

"The harvest hasn't been good this year, Jed. Money's tight."

"So your answer is no." Jen said for him.

"Can yuh give me another six months? I promise yuh I'll do my best to get it for yuh"

"I've already given you six. I won't wait any longer."

Abel's eyes widened. "What're yuh gonna do? You're not gonna kill me, are yuh Jed?"

Jed shook his head. "I wouldn't do that, Abel. No, I'm going to take your daughter."

Abel took a step back in surprise. "What do yuh mean?"

"I need a woman to cook and clean around the place. The house is turning into a pigsty. From what I've seen of Annie, she's capable of just about anything, so I want her to become housekeeper for three months. In return, I'll cancel your debt."

Abel was quiet for a while. Jed remained silent, letting him mull over his offer. In all truth, Abel would be stupid to turn him down.

"And what if I don't agree? What if Annie doesn't agree?" Abel said warily.

"If you don't, I'll take enough of your horses to pay the debt. I've waited long enough. I'm not an unreasonable man, Abel; you know that. We all have our own debts and expenses. When I lent you that money for the seeds, you said you'd pay me back at the end of the harvest. You didn't."

Abel rubbed his forehead. "But what am I gonna do without my daughter to help around the place?"

"She can come back once a week to aid you. That's all. The rest of the time, she's mine."

"You ain't gonna hurt her, are yuh? 'Cause if yuh do, I'll hunt yuh down myself!" Abel said, his eyes narrowing with anger.

"I would never hurt her, Abel. You know me too well for that." He looked at him astutely. "So, do we have a deal?"

"I don't really have much choice, do I?"

"Not really, no."

"Very well, I'll have a word with her. If she agrees, that's fine, but if she doesn't, I'll find another way to pay yuh back. Somethin' that doesn't involve yuh takin' my horses." Abel said, reluctantly agreeing to his terms.

In three months' time, with a winter of hard work under Annie's belt, his debt would be paid. Jed remounted his horse and looked down at him. "I'll leave you to tell Annie, and I'll return in a week with the wagon. Make sure she's ready."

. . ⚕ . .

Annie heard the kitchen door open, just as she was taking the stew out of the oven. She placed the big pot on the table and turned around to look at her father. "What did Jed Wheeler want, Pa?"

Something about his expression made her stop dead still. "What is it, Pa? What's happened?"

"Come into the living room, Annie. There's somethin' I have to tell yuh."

She threw down her tea towel and followed him into the other room. He stopped in front of the fireplace and, placing one hand on the mantel, looked down into the flames.

"I've let yuh down, Annie."

Her heart almost stopped. What on earth had he done?

"I tried my best," he continued, "I really did, but I couldn't pay Jed the money I owed him."

Annie's eyes widened. She knew her father had borrowed money for seed after a bad harvest but hadn't realized how deep a hole they were in. She clasped her hands together nervously. "But I thought you'd paid him back?"

Her father shook his head sadly. "No, I should've told yuh before, but the time never seemed right."

"So what happens now?" Annie paced back and forth on the little rug. "Is he gonna take our house? Is that what he wants? We don't have anything else."

"He wants you."

Annie stopped pacing, and her jaw fell open. "Me?"

Her father nodded. "He wants yuh to work for him for three months, and then he'll cancel the debt."

Annie sat down on the nearest chair, her mind working fast. Jed wanted her to work for him. "What does he want me to do?"

"Cook and clean."

If it meant cancelling the debt, she could do that. Couldn't she? "But how will you cope on your own, Pa?"

"He said yuh can come back once a week to help out here. The rest of the time yuh have to be at his ranch."

She sat quietly for a moment in contemplation, nibbling on her fingernail. Jed was intimidating, and being in close proximity with him might prove to be a bit daunting. But their debt would be cancelled, and what was three months? She would be back in time to help with the next spring planting, and she could come back and help her father every week.

Besides which, she saw no other choice.

"I'm truly sorry, Annie." Her father said quietly. "And I understand if yuh don't want to go. I won't put any pressure on yuh. We can find some other way to pay him. He said he could take some of our horses."

Annie immediately leapt up and went over to hug him. "Pa, he ain't having our horses, that's for sure. Look, we can't raise that sort of money, so I don't want you to worry about it any more. I'll go to him. It's only for three months, and if it means our debt will be cancelled, then I can do it."

He patted her back. "You're a good daughter, Annie. Even when your pa lets yuh down."

"Oh, these things happen, Pa. Ain't for you to worry about now. I don't mind helping out, and three months will go by in the blink of an eye. Plus, I can come back every week to help you here." She kissed him on the cheek. "Come on, let's have dinner."

Although she said the words so confidently, it was mainly to appease her pa and put his mind at rest. Inside, she was quite daunted at the prospect of spending three months at Jed Wheeler's ranch. But as fate would have it, that's exactly what she was going to do.

· · ❧ · ·

A *week later*
Annie paced the living room, every now and then stopping to look out of the window. Jed was due today, and her bags were packed and ready to go.

Oh, Lord, she was so nervous!

Over the last week, she'd had a couple of occasions where she'd been close to backing out but the stakes were too high. The only alternative was giving Jed some of their thoroughbred horses, and that wasn't going to happen. Uh-uh.

No, she had to do this. Perhaps under Jed's stern exterior there was a soft heart? She pulled a face. He didn't look like he had a soft heart. Not at all.

A noise made her look up, and the man himself came into view, his wagon coming to a halt outside the front gate.

She closed her eyes for a moment to calm her nerves. Oh, Lord. She felt sick.

Swallowing hard, she straightened her back and walked over to the front door. Her father was already out the front talking to him. She stopped dead still for a moment to take a real good look at the man she would be living with for three months.

There was no denying that he cut a handsome figure. He was at least a head taller than her father, who was by no means a small man. But not only was Jed tall, but his shoulders were broad and strong, giving an overall appearance of strength.

He swivelled his head to look at her, his eyes locking with hers, and she felt colour fill her face at being caught in such blatant perusal.

.. ⚘ ..

Jed studied the petite little blonde that he'd come to collect. She was a pretty girl. Her curves were all in the right place, and her long blonde hair glistened in the winter sun. Her eyes were intelligent and a vibrant shade of blue.

But that wasn't why he wanted her at his ranch. He'd heard rumours of what a capable girl she was, and it was exactly what he needed.

His sister, Mary, had taken off four months ago. Run off with a travelling salesman of all things. He'd told her not to trust a man like that—he advised her until he was blue in the face—but it hadn't mattered a damn. She'd just left a note and gone.

He didn't have time for cleaning and the like. His ranch hands were the same. Food on the table had consisted of anything they could scrape together. None of them had a clue how to cook a decent meal.

As for cleaning and tidying, well, one look at his place, and Annie would most probably try and run back to her pa. But he was going to make sure that didn't happen. He needed her, and if she wanted her pa's debt cleared, then she'd have to tow the line.

He walked up to her, his eyes keenly assessing her flushed cheeks. "Afternoon, Annie. Your pa told me that you've agreed to come. I'm mighty glad you have."

"Oh?"

He nodded. "We need a woman's touch about the place." He didn't elaborate. He didn't want her to change her mind. Enough said. "Is this all your luggage?"

He looked down at the two carpet bags by her feet.

When she nodded, he picked them up and strode back to the wagon, calling gruffly over his shoulder, "Say your goodbyes; I want to get back before nightfall."

. . ✿ . .

Lily trembled slightly at his tone. He was so intimidating, and it didn't seem to be a front; it just came naturally to him. Her father came to stand in front of her, his eyes sad. "If yuh want to back out, Annie, it won't bother me none."

She patted his arm, "No, Pa. I've made my mind up. Besides, I'll be back next week to visit. Don't you worry none about me."

She kissed him on the cheek and, taking a deep breath, headed over to the wagon. Jed was waiting for her, and before she could say a word, he placed his hands around her small waist and lifted her straight up onto the bench seat. Reaching for a blanket, he wrapped it over her lap and tucked it behind her.

The close proximity was a little disconcerting, and she risked a quick glance at his face. His eyes were a deep hazel framed by dark lashes. They were quite mesmerising and gulping; she realised she was unintentionally staring. Again.

Quickly, she looked down, but not before she heard a deep chuckle. Oh, so he found her amusing, did he? She bristled and pursed her lips. That was the second time he'd caught her staring.

As they set off across the darkening prairie, Annie looked around to see her pa standing out in front of the house. He looked so alone that she wanted to rush back and hug him. Closing her eyes for a moment to quell her emotions, she turned back to the horizon. She should learn to worry less, but it was hard. After all, he was all she had.

Their neighbour, Emiline Tompkins, or Emmy to her friends, was going to call in every now and then to see how her pa was faring. She was a widow, and Annie secretly thought she was sweet on her pa. Not that he noticed. But just knowing she would be there for him made Annie's current task a lot easier.

As they rode, Annie stole glances at Jed as he sat beside her, his workroughened hands gripping the reins with ease. Though his reputation preceded him as a stern, no-nonsense man, she couldn't help but admire his profile. There weren't many men that handsome in her neck of the woods.

They soon arrived at Jed's large ranch house. "You'll have your chores outlined tomorrow," he said gruffly as he helped her down off the wagon, again putting his hands around her waist and lifting her onto the ground as though she weighed no more than a feather.

He picked up her bags and then led her up the wooden steps into the house. It was dark inside, and apart from the fire with its embers burning low, she couldn't make out much.

Lighting a candle, Jed swiftly showed her up the stairs and into a small bedroom. "I'll leave you to get settled in. Come down when you're ready in the morning, and I'll introduce you to everyone." He left the candle with her, and the next minute, he was gone.

Annie stood for a moment and looked around the room. In the candlelight, it looked quite cosy. The bed was made, and there was a pitcher of water on a small table in one corner. But it was cold. Damn cold.

Opening one of her carpet bags, she drew out some clothes and laid them on the bed, sifting through them until she found her night attire. With lightning speed, she undressed, throwing on her nightdress and quickly placed a shawl around her shoulders for extra warmth. She was going to need it!

Climbing beneath the covers, she snuggled down and curled into a ball, trying to keep her body warm. Too exhausted to ponder what lay ahead, Annie quickly blew out the candle and fell into a deep sleep.

About the Author

Maryse Dawson was born in England but now lives in western France with her family - a husband, three children and two cats. When she's not writing she spends her time visiting the beaches and surrounding countryside. She has always enjoyed reading romances and loves history so began writing a few years ago to include domestic discipline in her stories. An alpha male - a feisty woman and adventures that will keep you turning the pages!

Read more at https://www.facebook.com/maryse.dawson.5.